CATECHESIS NUMERIS MUSICIS INCLUSA
and
SCHÖNE UND AUSERLESENE
DEUDSCHE UND LATEINISCHE GEISTLICHE GESENGE

RECENT RESEARCHES IN THE MUSIC OF THE RENAISSANCE

James Haar and Howard Mayer Brown, general editors

A-R Editions, Inc., publishes six quarterly series—

Recent Researches in the Music of the Middle Ages and Early Renaissance,
Margaret Bent, general editor;

Recent Researches in the Music of the Renaissance,
James Haar and Howard Mayer Brown, general editors;

Recent Researches in the Music of the Baroque Era,
Robert L. Marshall, general editor;

Recent Researches in the Music of the Classical Era,
Eugene K. Wolf, general editor;

Recent Researches in the Music of the Nineteenth and Early Twentieth Centuries,
Jerald C. Graue, general editor;

Recent Researches in American Music,
H. Wiley Hitchcock, general editor—

which make public music that is being brought to light
in the course of current musicological research.

Each volume in the *Recent Researches* is devoted
to works by a single composer or to a single genre of composition,
chosen because of its potential interest to scholars and performers,
and prepared for publication according to the standards that govern
the making of all reliable historical editions.

Subscribers to this series, as well as patrons of subscribing institutions,
are invited to apply for information about the "Copyright-Sharing Policy"
of A-R Editions, Inc., under which the contents of this volume
may be reproduced free of charge for study or performance.

Correspondence should be addressed:

A-R EDITIONS, INC.
315 West Gorham Street
Madison, Wisconsin 53703

RECENT RESEARCHES IN THE MUSIC OF THE RENAISSANCE • VOLUME XXXIX

Mattheus Le Maistre

CATECHESIS NUMERIS MUSICIS INCLUSA
and
SCHÖNE UND AUSERLESENE DEUDSCHE UND LATEINISCHE GEISTLICHE GESENGE

Edited by Donald Gresch

A-R EDITIONS, INC. • MADISON

ISSN 0486-123X

ISBN 0-89579-160-9

Library of Congress Cataloging in Publication Data:
Le Maistre, Mattheus, d. 1577.
[Catechesis numeris musicis inclusa]
Catechesis numeris musicis inclusa ; and, Schöne
und auserlesene deudsche und lateinische geistliche
Gesenge.

   (Recent researches in the music of the
Renaissance , ISSN 0486-123X ; v. 39)
   Part-songs ; principally for 3 voices.
   Latin words (in the 1st work) ; German or Latin
words (in the 2nd) ; English translations on p. xix.
   Originally published: Nürnberg : Montanus and
Neuber, 1563 (1st work) ; Dresden : G. Bergen, 1577
(2nd work)
   Includes bibliographic references.
   1. Part-songs, Sacred.   2. Part-songs, German.
I. Gresch, Donald C.   II. Le Maistre, Mattheus, d.
1577. Schöne und auserlesene deudsche und
lateinische geistliche Gesenge. 1981.
III. Title.   IV. Title: Schöne und auserlesene
deudsche und lateinische geistliche Gesenge.
V. Series.
M2.R2384   vol. 39   [M3.1]   81-17622
ISBN 0-89579-160-9   AACR2

Contents

Preface

The Composer

In 1554, Mattheus Le Maistre was appointed to the position of *Kapellmeister* at the Saxon electoral court in Dresden. From then until his death in 1577, court documents provide a fairly complete record of the events of his life. On the other hand, we know very little of his early life. There are, for example, only bits of evidence suggesting that Le Maistre was born in the Netherlands. In the Dresden court *Canntoreiordnung* of 1555, Elector August indicated that Le Maistre's predecessor in the position of *Kapellmeister*, Johann Walther, would be released from his duties "as soon as we have brought here a new *Kapellmeister* together with some apprentices and boys from the Netherlands."[1] Even more conclusive than this document is the composer's reference to himself as "Matthaeo le Meistre Belga" on the title page of his *Catechesis numeris musicis inclusa*, first published in 1559 (see Plate I).

There is no evidence that might suggest from whom Le Maistre may have had his musical training, but in the preface to the *Schöne und auserlesene Deudsche und Lateinische Geistliche Gesenge*, published in 1577, the composer made the significant comment that "the pursuit of music was not encouraged in my youth."[2]

Apart from these few references to his nationality and youthful activities, and despite the fact that a number of music historians have suggested various possibilities regarding Le Maistre's early life, there is very little evidence that indicates Le Maistre's whereabouts and professional activities before his appointment at the court in Dresden in 1554.[3] The only documentable suggestion thus far offered is Adolf Sandberger's contention that Le Maistre was a member of the Bavarian court chapel in Munich before his appointment to the Saxon electoral court at Dresden.[4] This supposition is based on the record of a certain "Mathesz" in the list of personnel in the Bavarian court chapel from the year 1552. This "Mathesz" is described in the chapel roll as a Netherlander, so he may have been identical with Mattheus Le Maistre. The next listing of the Bavarian court chapel personnel dates from 1557, and the "Mathesz" concerned is not mentioned. He must, then, have left the Bavarian court sometime between 1552 and 1557. If this was Le Maistre, that

date does not conflict with the date of his move to Dresden in 1554. A number of other circumstances further corroborate Sandberger's claim. First, the overwhelming majority of Le Maistre's Catholic music (Masses, Responsories, Latin motets, and Mass Propers) is preserved in the manuscript choirbooks that originally belonged to the Bavarian court chapel. These manuscripts, which are now part of the holdings of the Bayerische Staatsbibliothek in Munich, are unique to that library. However, a few other European libraries do have manuscripts of other works by Le Maistre that are not duplicated in the archives of the Bayerische Staatsbibliothek. Second, Julius Maier, in his catalogue of the old music manuscripts in the Bavarian court library in Munich, stated that the manuscripts of Le Maistre's polyphonic Mass Proper cycle were copied by Ludwig Daser's scribe.[5] This conclusion is significant because Daser was a member of the Bavarian court chapel for most of his life, and he even served as its *Kapellmeister* during the reign of Duke Albrecht V (1552–1559). Therefore, Daser's scribe certainly must have known and had direct contact with the other members of the chapel, and he also could have copied music for them. Maier's identification of the scribe of Le Maistre's music strongly supports Sandberger's supposition that the "Mathesz" listed in the 1552 roll of the Bavarian court chapel was Le Maistre. Presumably, then, Le Maistre was employed at the Bavarian court chapel in Munich sometime prior to 1554, and it was for this organization that he wrote his music for Catholic services.

Le Maistre's tenure as *Kapellmeister* at the Saxon electoral court chapel in Dresden began in the autumn of 1554. The first document giving evidence of his presence there is a letter he wrote in October of that year acknowledging his receipt of the musical archives of the chapel.[6] Shortly thereafter, Le Maistre's official appointment, together with details regarding his specific duties and his salary, were set forth in the *Canntoreiordnung* of 1 January 1555.[7] According to this document, Le Maistre was paid a salary of 240 *gulden* annually and reimbursed for the expenses he incurred in caring for the choirboys who lived with him. He was also provided with a new court uniform each year and enjoyed free meals whenever the elector held banquets at the court. Le Maistre's professional duties as *Kapell-*

meister included giving the choirboys music lessons, rehearsing the choir and directing its performances, and providing music for the numerous religious services and secular social functions that graced the ritual of life at the Saxon court. To this end Le Maistre composed a large corpus of music during his twenty-three years in Dresden, including a setting of the Latin Mass Ordinary, a setting of the Latin *Catechesis*, a huge collection of sacred and secular *Teutsche Geseng* for four and five voices, a collection of German and Latin *Geistliche Gesenge*, and many Latin motets and other miscellaneous pieces.

Even though Le Maistre appears to have executed his duties at the court with competence, on 22 December 1565 he petitioned Elector August for permission to be released from the obligations involved in the administration of the chapel.[8] According to this document, Le Maistre was severely disabled by gout and an accidental fall he sustained in the church at Torgau. He also complained of insufficient income and asked the elector for a pension and a place to live for the rest of his life. In return, he promised to continue to compose music for the elector even though he could no longer manage the administration of the entire chapel organization.

The elector granted Le Maistre's request for a pension,[9] but Le Maistre was not officially released from his duties in the chapel until 12 February 1568, when Antonio Scandello was appointed his successor. From then until his death in 1577, Le Maistre remained at the court, assisting in the activities of the chapel when he could, composing new music, and preparing several collections of his music for publication. According to the archives of the Saxon court, Le Maistre died sometime shortly after 22 January 1577.

The Music

The CATECHESIS *and* GESENGE *as products of the Saxon Court*

The *Catechesis numeris musicis inclusa* (1559) and the *Deudsche und Lateinische Geistliche Gesenge* (1577) represent, respectively, the first and last music Le Maistre published during the time he was in Dresden. Despite the fact that they were composed eighteen years apart, these two collections of songs are related by two common features. First, the pieces in the two collections are, with only two exceptions (where *si placet* parts are added), scored for a three-voice ensemble that lacks a real bass voice. The three voices of the *Catechesis* are labeled Primus Discantus, Secundus Discantus, and Pars Infima,

while those of the *Gesenge* are called Suprema Vox, Media Vox, and Infima Vox. Second, the texts of the "Benedictio mensae" and the "Gratiarum actio" of the *Catechesis* reappear, in German translations and in different musical settings, as the first two pieces of the *Gesenge*.

The *Catechesis* is dedicated to the heir apparent, Alexander, who died in 1565, and the *Gesenge* is dedicated to Alexander's brother Christian, who succeeded August as Saxon elector in 1588. Even though the two works are specifically dedicated to Elector August's sons, their prefaces clearly indicate that Le Maistre intended both collections to be used by the choirboys and other youngsters at the court as well. These prefaces are informative and interesting enough to warrant translation in full. The preface to the *Catechesis* reads as follows:

Greetings and salutations to the most illustrious prince, lord duke August, elector and archmarshal of the Holy Roman Empire, duke of Saxony, etc., and to the son of my most clement lord, lord duke Alexander.

Great is the glory, pleasing to God, and extending to all posterity, that there are still princes, who through the kindness of God in this troublesome old age of the world, are eager to pursue the glory of God without pretense and feigned zeal. I am not now speaking about others lest I seem to assume judgment of things placed beyond my grasp, but I am speaking about you, renowned Alexander, who are rightly moved by the distinguished piety of your parents to a keen pursuit of piety even from your tender youth. Praise and glory to God, Father of our Lord Jesus Christ, who under your father, my most gracious lord, is still preserving the true and uncorrupted doctrine of the Law and the Gospel in Meissen, against all insults and sloth of the devil and those who have abandoned the faith. This also we pray, with ardent prayers, that there may gather together forever in this region an army of men believing and teaching the true doctrine of the Law and the Gospel.

So that I may in a few words come to the point, which I feel I must bring to the attention of your serenity, I offer this Catechism, which is appropriate for the age of your highness, and which is written in the true form and order, and set to music in a style most proper for your tender age. Through the encouragement of Magister Nikolaus Selnecker (I cannot keep this a secret), I first came to this [Catechism] so that the boys in our musical choir, in particular, might use this form. Since I believed that this study of mine would be pleasing to good men, through the encouragement of Selnecker and others, I permitted it to be published not because I was offering something written in a sophisticated style, since I know this music is for children, but for the sake of piety which is dear to the heart of your highness, as I have said. I do not doubt that your highness, as a good and fair man, will approve of my work. And I hope that unprejudiced judges, who will understand my intentions, will be fair to me. I do not think I should speak about others, for each is entitled to his own opinion. I commend your highness to God that he may preserve and keep safe the unending succession of your highness.

Dedicated to your highness,
Mattheus Le Maistre, Chapelmaster.[10]

The somewhat more verbose preface to the *Gesenge* of 1577 alludes to the problem with gout that Le Maistre experienced toward the end of his life. It reads as follows:

To the most illustrious prince and lord, lord Christian, duke of Saxony, the son of the most serene and powerful prince elector August, the landgrave of Thuringia and the margrave of Meissen, to his own most clement lord he gives the highest greeting.

In the Church of God, in the name of the undivided trinity, most illustrious prince and most clement lord, it has been customary to begin the holy office and divine assemblies with songs and even with most devout prayers in the custom of the apostles, as we read in Acts. For God has gifted man also with the true awareness of the numbers of harmony, and has wished man to understand the heavenly doctrine and divine praises in the celebration of his name and our own salvation, so that the sacred words and holy doctrines may penetrate more deeply the minds of the listeners so that more ardent stimuli toward piety may be kindled in the hearts of the faithful, as the types of songs of men such as Moses, Joshua, David, Asaph, Solomon, Isaiah, Jeremiah, etc., show.

In this last age, and through the expressed will of God, this golden age, such songs which have been joined by nature to our souls in all tongues (as D. Basilius mentions) have increased in the use of the churches, so that the praise of the almighty God may be eternal and his glory forever. For D. Luther, the German Orpheus, of blessed memory, has imbued the Psalms of David, which are especially suitable for the sensibilities of men, with his own very vital music, so that all nations to whom our language is known may celebrate and praise [God] as they delight in them. Their piety and zeal we certainly do approve of and rightfully imitate.

For to sing Psalms is the gift of angels, a heavenly state and a spiritual unguent.

Inasmuch as the pursuit of music was not encouraged in me from my youth, and inasmuch as I lost the patrimony of my family, so that I might lessen in some measure the torture of my illness, I have composed these *Tricinia*, and in this way I have sung a new song to David's descendant, my Christ and Savior, the only Redeemer of our souls. Troubled for a long time and in a great degree by the gout, I could not and did not exercise to a greater extent my intellectual talents.

In my choice of a patron whom my study of music does not displease and who will not scorn [it], most illustrious prince, lord Maecenas most clement, besides your illustrious highness, I know no one; I am not able to please you with learned songs: but I offer them to those studious young men who, instead of study, at thanksgiving time both before and after dinner, wish to sing them with me.

So that I may not be accused of the basest charge of ingratitude (for I am totally indebted to the illustrious house of Saxony), I offer and dedicate this insignificant and mean work to your illustrious highness, which your illustrious highness kindly deigns to accept from me and which I earnestly seek and entreat you to accept. It befits a man, as Sophocles teaches, to remember if something pleasing has happened to him: for gratitude always begets gratitude, and he who remembers a kindness done to him will in turn be a generous man. And Cicero says: For jurors, although I wish to be gifted with all virtues, there is nothing which I would prefer than that I be and seem to be grateful.

To the triune God I commend your illustrious highness and the entire lands of Saxony. Dated 1 January, A. D. 1577.

The servant of your illustrious highness, Mattheus Le Maistre, Senior Chapelmaster.[11]

The *Catechesis* sets only the texts of the five principal parts of the Catechism (the Ten Commandments, Apostle's Creed, Lord's Prayer, and statements on Baptism and Communion) and the two traditional mealtime prayers originating in Roman Catholic usage. The assumption[12] that Le Maistre drew the texts of his *Catechesis* directly from one of the available Latin versions of Luther's *Small Catechism* is open to question. First, Le Maistre's *Catechesis* presents only the traditional authoritative statement of each of the items, omitting all the explanatory commentary that Luther included in his *Small Catechism*. Second, neither the general contents nor all of the textual details of Le Maistre's *Catechesis* correspond exactly to any one of the earliest Latin editions of Luther's *Small Catechism*.[13] Finally, in the preface to his *Catechesis*, Le Maistre never mentions Luther's name, nor once overtly refers to the Lutheran Reformation. If this is the preface to a musical setting of Luther's *Small Catechism*, the omission of Luther's name seems curious considering the significant role the Saxon electors played in protecting both the person and the work of Martin Luther.

Besides Elector August and his son Alexander, to whom the work is dedicated, the only other person mentioned in the preface to the *Catechesis* is Nikolaus Selnecker. Selnecker held the position of Court Preacher at the Saxon court between the years 1558 and 1564, and is known in the annals of the history of the Reformation for the Philippist bent of his teachings and for the role he played in the feud between the orthodox Lutheran Ernestine and the Philippist Albertine branches of the house of Wettin. The Albertine Philippists embraced some of the teachings of Philipp Melanchthon, while the Ernestines propounded orthodox Lutheranism. The details of this unpleasant episode in the history of the Saxon court are too intricate to bear full rehearsal here. It will suffice to note that during the early years of the Reformation, Elector August, often following the recommendations of Melanchthon, in whom he placed great trust, unwittingly appointed a large number of Philippist theologians to important positions in the churches and universities in Albertine Saxony. On the recommendation of Melanchthon, in January of 1558 August appointed Nikolaus Selnecker to the position of Court Preacher at his electoral court in Dresden. Apparently August was pleased with the work of his new preacher, and a year later Selnecker's duties were expanded to include training the boys in the choir and tutoring the elector's young son, Alexander.

In the execution of these pedagogical duties, Selnecker certainly must have needed a Catechism from which his young charges could learn the tenets of the faith. However, this Catechism must also have accorded with Selnecker's Philippist beliefs, which, in some instances, ran counter to orthodox Lutheran teachings. For example, two of the more important areas of controversy between the orthodox Lutherans and the Philippists were Luther's Doctrine of the Real Presence and his stand on confession. Luther expressed his ideas on these matters in the exegetical portions of his *Small Catechism*, and he even included an entire special section on confession. Luther's *Small Catechism* was not entirely in accord with the Philippists' views.

Selnecker's alteration of any of Luther's statements in the *Small Catechism* would have been tantamount to the admission of his divergence from orthodox Lutheran views. Therefore, Selnecker probably prepared a version of the Catechism whose contents were confined to the authoritative five principal parts of the Catechism that contained nothing objectionable to Lutherans or to Philippists. To this basic core he could have added the theologically innoxious table prayers because his duties would have included teaching these prayers to the choirboys. Thus, it may have been a version of the Catechism prepared by Selnecker that Le Maistre set to music and published in 1559. In his preface to the printed edition of the *Catechesis*, Le Maistre openly acknowledged Selnecker's participation in its preparation:

> . . . Through the encouragement of Magister Nikolaus Selnecker (I cannot keep this a secret) I first came to this [Catechism] so that the boys in our musical choir, in particular, might use this form.

Immediately before this acknowledgement, Le Maistre referred to this *Catechesis* as one "which is written in the true form and order." These direct references to both Selnecker and to a special form of the Catechism suggest that the text of Le Maistre's musical *Catechesis* is not literally that of Luther's *Small Catechism*, but another version of it in use at the Saxon court.

In 1564, only one year after the publication of the second edition of Le Maistre's setting of the *Catechesis*, Selnecker was forced to leave the court because of political embroilments. Finally, in 1574, Elector August became aware of the Philippist infiltration of electoral Saxony, forthwith expelled all Philippists, and at least nominally returned the entire Wettin domain to the orthodox Lutheran faith.

Le Maistre's tenure at the Saxon court coincided with the duration of the Philippist controversy there. During this period the court was both theologically and politically one of the hottest spots in all of Western Europe. What Le Maistre's personal stand in the controversy may have been will perhaps never be known. There can be little doubt that he was aware of the battle of wits raging around him, and the influence of this feud may be traced in the prefaces to the music he published during this period. His preface to the huge collection of *Geistliche und Weltliche Teutsche Geseng*, published in Wittenberg in 1566, like that of the earlier *Catechesis*, contains not a single reference to Martin Luther or to anything generally Lutheran. Indeed, the main thesis treated in the preface to the 1566 publication turns on the desirability, even the necessity, of good music in the church. In support of this thesis Le Maistre refers to both Testaments of the Bible and cites pagan authors such as Pindar and Aristotle as well. The omission of references to any of Luther's views on this crucial topic was most likely the result of the presence throughout Saxony of

Philippist partisans whose sensibilities he would have offended by quoting the Reformer directly.

With the rise to power of the fanatically orthodox Lutheran Duke John William in Ernestine Saxony in 1567, the Philippists in Albertine Saxony began to lose ground in their theological feud with the Lutherans. Soon the Philippists were defeated and, as noted earlier, in 1574 Elector August officially banished them from all of Saxony. Characteristically, in the prefatory statements to Le Maistre's next two collections of music, one published in 1570 and the other in 1577, Martin Luther is cited as one of the principal authorities in support of the composer's statements on music in the church. The following sentences drawn from the preface to the 1570 *Sacrum Cantionum* demonstrate this new emphasis:

> It is not easy to say to what extent the songs of Dr. M. Luther and other pious men (whose memories be blessed) serve the church today, since it is known that the sum total of Christian doctrine is contained in them, and that the youth and the common people could more easily be brought to the true faith through these melodies. For this reason even that revered man Dr. M. Luther has attributed to music the next place and honor after theology because, he said, she was her servant and contributed in no small way to the preservation of the purity of the doctrine.[14]

And finally, in the preface to his last collection, the three-voice *Gesenge*, published in the year of his death, Le Maistre paid Luther the following supreme compliment:

> For D. Luther, the German Orpheus, . . . has imbued the Psalms of David . . . with his own very vital music, so that all nations to whom our language is known may celebrate and praise [God] as they delight in them.

The overtly orthodox Lutheran character of the 1577 *Gesenge* is corroborated by its contents. Out of the twenty German songs in this collection exactly half are polyphonic arrangements of chorales originally written by Luther himself. The forms and styles of texts by other authors conform to the chorale tradition established by Luther.

The Musical Style of the CATECHESIS and GESENGE

Three clearly defined musical styles are represented in the *Catechesis* and the *Gesenge*: homophonic; canonic; and contrapuntally imitative.

The first five sections of the *Catechesis* are basically homophonic, with the texts underlaid syllabically in all the voices. Departures from the prevailing chordal texture are rare, and, when they do occur, they usually amount to little more than the embellishment of the cadential suspension typical of music of this period (see, for example, no. I, mm. 30, 35–36, 50–51, and elsewhere). This severely homophonic style, which permits clear declamation of the text, was undoubtedly occasioned by the didactic purpose of these settings.

In striking contrast to the textural simplicity of the first five pieces of the *Catechesis*, the two table prayers exploit one of the most sophisticated of all compositional techniques—strict canon. Since the text of each prayer consists of two parts, Le Maistre divided the music of each prayer into two units, so that altogether there are four canons, two at the unison for no. VI, "Benedictio mensae," and two at the perfect fifth below for no. VII, "Gratiarum actio." In these pieces, even the style of the non-canonic Pars Infima is similar to that of the canonic voices. Thus, the overall impression is more that of imitative motet texture, two voices of which are incidentally in canon, than it is of an independent two-voice canon accompanied by a third non-canonic voice. In fact, often the temporal distances between the canonic entries are long enough to permit the Pars Infima to enter between the *dux* and *comes* of the canon. This technique destroys rather than enhances the effect of the strict canon between the two upper voices.

Finally, the musical style of the majority of works in the *Gesenge* is imitative counterpoint. In this style successive phrases of text are set to musical subjects that, in turn, are presented imitatively in all the voices, creating a musical texture composed of successive points of imitation. Usually a piece has as many imitative points as it has lines of text.

Many of the pieces in the 1577 collection of *Gesenge* are based on pre-existent chorale melodies. In these pieces the *cantus prius factus* may permeate all the voices (see, for example, no. XVI), or it may be treated as a real *cantus firmus* that dominates one voice and provides motivic material for the remaining voices (as in no. VI). It is possible to identify the chorale melodies that provide the bases for many of the *Gesenge*, and these melodic sources are cited in the Critical Notes. However, it is much more difficult to identify pre-existent melodies for most of the *Catechesis*. In this work the setting of the "Pater noster" is certainly based on the traditional chant for this liturgical item (the melody appears in the Secundus Discantus). However, Kade has contended that "Le Maistre based almost all movements [of the *Catechesis*] on originally Catholic Gregorian *cantus firmi*, which subsequently were taken into the Protestant [liturgy]."[15] Kade then cites only the little unison incipit of no. I, "Decem Praecepta Dei," as an example of a Gregorian chant, and he gives no source for it. While the overall character of this melodic incipit is reminiscent of Gregorian chant, its origin has not yet been traced to any source other than Le Maistre's *Catechesis* itself. There is a Protestant chorale[16] based on a paraphrase of the texts of the Ten Commandments, that, like Le Maistre's setting in the *Catechesis*, also begins with an intonation, "Dies sind die heil'gen zehn Gebot." However, the starkly monotonous character of the chorale incipit is so different from the incipit of Le Maistre's setting of the Decalogue that the likelihood of a direct relationship between them as well as the probability of their derivation from a common Gregorian source is very remote. A search for the melodic sources of the remainder of the pieces in the *Catechesis* has yielded similarly negative results.[17] Even though the overall musical effect of these settings does, in certain ways, approximate the fluid and sometimes austere character of Gregorian chant, this fact alone does not support the general assumption that the works in Le Maistre's *Catechesis* are based on Gregorian melodies.

Generally the music of Le Maistre's *Catechesis* and *Gesenge* reflects characteristics of both Franco-Flemish and German national styles. Typically Franco-Flemish are, for example, the imitative polyphonic texture, the canonic techniques, and the through-composed structures of many of these pieces. On the other hand, the pre-existent German chorale tunes used as *cantus firmi* betray the strong influence of the German polyphonic *Lied*. Also typically German are such technical features as occasional harsh dissonances and angular voice-leading.

The music of both the *Catechesis* and *Gesenge* is firmly rooted in the modal system. This, along with an unusually large proportion of vertical sonorities lacking harmonic thirds, gives many of these pieces in these two collections an austerely anachronistic ring.

The Sources

This edition of Le Maistre's *Catechesis numeris musicis inclusa* is based on the second edition published in Nuremberg in 1563 (RISM A, 1, L 1842) by the firm of Montanus and Neuber. A complete set of partbooks of the 1563 print is in the Bayerische Staatsbibliothek in Munich. The present edition of the *Catechesis* was prepared from microfilm copies of these partbooks. An incomplete set of partbooks (lacking the Media Vox) of the second edition is lo-

cated in the Sächsische Landesbibliothek in Dresden. Except for a single copy of the Pars Infima preserved in the British Library (see Plates I and II), all traces of the first (1559) edition of the *Catechesis*, also published by Montanus and Neuber (RISM A, 1, L 1841), appear to be lost. A comparison of the 1559 and the 1563 editions of the Pars Infima reveals that the later edition slavishly reproduces the first edition—including the errors. The 1563 edition might more accurately be regarded as a second printing rather than as a fresh edition.

The first and only edition of Le Maistre's *Deudsche und Lateinische Geistliche Gesenge* was published by Gimel Bergen in Dresden in 1577 (RISM A, 1, L 1845). The only known complete set of partbooks is in the Ratsschulbibliothek in Zwickau, and films of this copy provide the source of the present modern edition.

Although the present volume represents the first modern publication of the entire contents of Le Maistre's *Catechesis* and *Gesenge* since the sixteenth century, a number of individual pieces from both collections were reprinted in various anthologies published after about 1850. These concordant editions are listed in the Critical Notes for each piece.

Editorial Methods

Treatment of Musical Text

Each of the primary sources of Le Maistre's *Catechesis* and *Gesenge* consists of a set of three printed partbooks. In the present edition, score format is used. The variety of soprano, alto, tenor, and bass clefs occurring in the sources is replaced with the three clefs now in common use: the G-clef on the second line is used for treble parts; the G-clef with a joined 8 beneath it on the second line is used for tenor parts; and the F-clef on the fourth line is used for bass parts. Original note values are halved, except for final longs whose values are adjusted to coincide with the final notes in the other parts. Final longs in the source always carry fermatas in the transcriptions. Except for a single example of triple proportion in the middle of no. XXII of the *Gesenge*, the only two mensuration signs found in the sources for both the *Gesenge* and the *Catechesis* are C and ¢. Although the second of these signs at one time indicated proportional diminution, in these sources both signs appear to be used interchangeably, and occasionally both appear at random (possibly erroneously) in different voices of the same piece (for example, in the source of *Gesenge* nos. XI, XIII, and XXI). In this edition both of these mensuration signs are replaced with the modern signature $\frac{2}{2}$, with no proportional reduction for those parts originally carrying the sign ₵. Measure bars, not found in the original sources, have been placed in the transcriptions; these bars act only as visual guides and do not necessarily imply a regular, recurrent accent.

The second and third sections of multi-sectional pieces in the *Gesenge* are untitled. Occasionally the source has cues such as "secunda pars sequitur" or "verte pro tertia parte" at the conclusions of some sections. These cues have not been reproduced in the edition.

Incipits in the edition show original clefs, mensuration signs, accidentals, initial rests, and the first note of each voice part. However, errors in the sources are corrected both in these incipits and in the transcriptions; these corrections are documented in the Critical Notes.

All other editorial alterations and amplifications are enclosed within square brackets. Any group of notes that appears as a ligature in the source is enclosed within a horizontal bracket, while broken horizontal brackets indicate the presence of coloration in the source.

The music of Le Maistre's *Catechesis* and *Gesenge* presents no new *musica ficta* problems. On the other hand, all of the usual problems of editorial accidentals encountered in most other music from around the middle of the sixteenth century are present with annoying consistency. Thus, the guidelines for the chromatic alteration of notes in this edition shed no new light on this old problem; rather, they represent some of the current practices of chromatic alteration that yield fairly acceptable results when applied to music of the mid-sixteenth century:

I. Cadential accidentals
   A. Raising a pitch with a sharp or natural in the penultimate chord of a cadence pattern (*subsemitonium modi*); this chromatic alteration is frequently suggested by the presence of the characteristic syncopated lower auxiliary-note cadential figure in one of the upper voices
   B. Occasionally lowering a pitch through B-flat or E-flat, usually in the lowest voice, in the penultimate chord of a cadence pattern; this method of creating the *clausula vera* is sometimes used in situations where raising the pitch of a note in an upper voice would create an undesirable dissonance. The addition of cadential accidentals has been limited to rhythmically unaccented notes that resolve to accented ones, and to cadential patterns that terminate phrases or other structurally decisive units (for example, conclusions

of points of imitation); exceptions to this, including internal cadences defining structural units smaller than phrases and structurally decisive cadences where no chromatic alterations are possible, are frequent enough to warrant mention

II. Correction of imperfect harmonic intervals
   A. *Mi contra fa*—lowering a pitch, usually E or B, with a flat to perfect an imperfect harmonic fifth or octave or, occasionally, to prevent successive false relations
   B. *Una nota supra la*—adding a flat to B or E when these notes occur in the characteristic upper auxiliary-note figure; the affected note is commonly approached and left scalewise

III. *Tierce de Picardie*—raising the harmonic third, with a sharp or natural, of the final cadence chord of a structurally decisive unit

IV. Lowering B or E with a flat to eliminate a melodic tritone

These principles of chromatic alteration have been applied only with careful consideration of their musical effect. Exceptions to the procedures outlined above were freely made (1) whenever the addition of an accidental to correct one situation would create another situation as undesirable as the one the added accidental was intended to correct and (2) whenever the added accidental would seriously alter the melody or modal character of a *cantus prius factus* or an imitative subject. (There are, however, noteworthy exceptions to this. See, for example, *Gesenge* no. XIIII, mm. 5–8 and elsewhere, where the addition of E-flats to preserve the original form of the *cantus firmus* would create undesirable harmonic dissonances.)

Treatment of Vocal Texts

The text underlay in the printed sources of Le Maistre's *Catechesis* and *Gesenge* is typically imprecise. Those pieces or sections thereof that are primarily syllabic, such as nos. I through V of the *Catechesis*, are less problematic than those in the melismatic style of, for example, nos. VI and VII of the *Catechesis*. Relevant to this problem is the interesting statement on the title page of the *Gesenge* that indicates that these songs were not only composed by Le Maistre, but were "also corrected and set in print by [Le Maistre] himself."[18] Kade has interpreted this statement to mean that the composer literally set the type from which the pages of this edition were printed.[19] Even though the composer was personally involved in the preparation of the printed edition of the *Gesenge*, the text underlay is as arbitrary as that found in the majority of sixteenth-century prints. Apparently, Renaissance composers themselves were as nonchalant about text underlay in the printed editions of their music as were the printers who usually set the type.

In the underlay of texts in the present editions of the *Catechesis* and *Gesenge*, the following general guidelines have been followed: (1) if the underlay as given in the source was logical, it was retained; (2) in those pieces based on preexistent chorale tunes, the underlay of the text beneath the phrases of the original tune has served as a guide to the underlay in the polyphonic arrangement; (3) attempts were made to achieve a consistency of text underlay in repetitions of phrases of music in either the same or different voices; (4) when the text underlay of a predominantly melismatic passage could be made smoother by readjusting it according to Zarlino's rules of text underlay, such adjustment was made;[20] (5) in all other cases the texts were realigned so as to achieve the best musical results; (6) word-division follows principles established in the sources. Indications of adjustments of text underlay are not given in the Critical Notes, although text repetitions indicated in the sources by the symbol *ij* are enclosed within square brackets.

The forms of both the Latin (complete *Catechesis* and nos. XXI–XXIIII of the *Gesenge*) and the German texts (nos. I–XX of the *Gesenge*) in this edition conform closely to those of the sources.

The orthography and syntax of the Latin texts are similar enough to those of classical Latin that, aside from replacing "u" with "v" in such words as "saluus," further modernization was unnecessary. The German texts of the *Gesenge* present quite another problem. The orthography and word-order of sixteenth-century and modern German are often different, and, ideally, the texts of an edition intended for use by present-day performers should conform to present-day principles of German orthography. However, the modernization of a sixteenth-century German text frequently changes its syllable count, grammatical cases, and word pronunciation, with the result that the text no longer fits its original musical setting. Thus, in many instances the music of a passage would have had to have been substantially altered by deleting or adding notes to accommodate the modernized form of the text.

Moreover, Le Maistre himself had problems with the orthographic variability of German. For example, when Le Maistre set the first line of no. IIII of the *Gesenge*, "Herr deinem Knecht, schaff jtzund recht," he arbitrarily added an extra "e" to the word "Herr," making it a two-syllable word and chang-

ing the initial weak accent on the monosyllabic "Herr" to a strong accent on "Herre" ("Hérrĕ déiněm Knécht"). Then he set this altered version of the first word to an accented semibreve followed by an unaccented minim. In the source, this setting of the first strophe of text is followed by the complete text of seven strophes printed as a poem. The syllable count and accent patterns of the first lines of all these strophes conform to the pattern of the unaltered version of the first line of the first strophe in which the word "Herr" is an unaccented monosyllable. Therefore, it is impossible to sing any of the subsequent strophes of text to Le Maistre's music without either adding a syllable to the first word of every subsequent strophe or deleting a note from the first line of the music.

There are additional problems in fitting the texts of the subsequent strophes to the music. In the second strophe the word "hüte" has one too many syllables, while in the sixth strophe the hemistich "erbarm dich" is one syllable too short. Finally, the complete text of no. IIII is printed only in the Pars Infima partbook. To perform these strophes, the choristers singing the two upper parts would have had to memorize either the words of all these strophes, or the music so that after singing the first strophe they could have moved to positions from which they could have seen the text in the Pars Infima books held by the other boys. Both alternatives are unlikely, and it seems reasonable to conclude that none except the first strophe was ever intended to be sung. The long paraphrase of Psalm 26 was included in the collection probably more for reasons of religious pedagogy than for reasons of musical exercise.

With few exceptions, spelling, capitalization, punctuation, and word-order of the original German texts are retained in this edition of the *Gesenge*. Editorial alterations have been tacitly made, and they are confined to the correction of typographical errors and to occasional changes in spelling and capitalization to achieve consistency within a single piece. The orthography and word-order in the texts of the German *Gesenge* are not so remote from modern German that present-day singers will have difficulty with them. However, in the sixteenth century, the *Umlaut* was not used as consistently as it is in modern German, and sometimes the equivalent sounds were spelled in other ways (for example, e = ä, je = ü). At other times the *Umlaut* was omitted altogether, creating forms of words that look incorrect according to modern practice (for example, "uber," "fur"), but which accurately reflect the variability of sixteenth-century usage. The only other word in the texts of the German *Gesenge* whose form may be unfamiliar is the "sich" in the first line of no. XIIII, "Ach Gott von Himel sich darein." This looks like the modern third person reflexive pronoun, but it is the phonetic spelling of "sieh," the second person singular imperative form of the verb "sehen."

Critical Notes

This critical commentary includes the following information: (1) an indication of the mode of the music; (2) the identification, where appropriate, of the *cantus prius factus* on which the polyphony is based, together with references to sources of the *cantus prius factus*; and (3) critical editorial notes. For full documentation of sources and editions cited by abbreviation in this section, see the List of Abbreviations in the Appendix on p. xxiii.

Catechesis

I. Decem Praecepta Dei
(1) Mixolydian. (2) Freely composed. (3) Intonation, Pars Infima, source has the clef on the second line. M. 28, note 2 and m. 29, notes 1 and 2, Secundus Discantus, rhythm is a dotted semibreve followed by a minim in the source.

II. Symbolum Apostolorum
(1) Ionian transposed. (2) Freely composed. (3) *First part*: M. 75, Pars Infima, note 1 is f in the source. Concordance: Kad*M*, appendix, pp. 18–20.

III. Oratio Dominica
(1) Dorian transposed. (2) Based on the traditional chant for the "Pater noster," Fa*MGG* 10: cols. 943–951. (3) M. 4, Pars Infima, note 2 is a breve in the source. M. 7, Pars Infima, note 3 is a breve in the source. M. 8, Pars Infima, note 1 is a breve in the source. M. 27, Pars Infima, note 3 is d in the source. M. 37, Pars Infima, note 2 is d in the source. Concordances: Kad*M*, appendix, pp. 16–17, and Mald*R*, I: 23–24.

IIII. De Baptismo
(1) Ionian transposed. (2) Freely composed.

V. De Coena Domini
(1) Ionian transposed. (2) Freely composed.

VI. Benedictio Mensae
(1) Ionian transposed. (2) Freely composed. (3) M. 11, Secundus Discantus, notes 3 and 4 are a semibreve in the source. The signs of congruence (ς) and the fermatas (⌒) found in the Primus Discantus merely indicate the beginnings and ends of the canonic *resolutio* (Secundus Discantus) and should be ignored in performance of the music.

VII. Gratiarum Actio
(1) Ionian transposed. (2) Freely composed. (3) *Second part*: M. 7, Secundus Discantus, note 2 is a' in the source. M. 14, Primus Discantus, note 5 is a fusa in the source. The signs of congruence (ς) and the fermatas (⌒) found in the Primus Discantus merely indicate the beginnings and ends of the canonic *resolutio* (Secundus Discantus) and should be ignored in performance of the music.

Gesenge

I. Das Benedicite
First part: (1) Dorian transposed. (2) Freely composed. (3) Incipit, Suprema Vox, the flat is in the fourth space in the source. *Second part*: (1) Dorian (or Aeolian) transposed. (2) Based on the traditional "Vater unser" chant melody of Ame*H*, 1, pt. 1, no. 345. *Third part*: (1) Aeolian transposed. (2) Freely composed. (3) M. 7, note 3–m. 14, note 2, Suprema Vox, the clef is on the second line in the source. Concordances: Ame*H*, 1, pt. 2, pp. 249–252, and Götz*C*, pp. 153–156.

II. Das Gratias
First part: (1) Aeolian transposed. (2) Freely composed. (3) Incipit, Infima Vox, source has a semibreve-rest following the mensuration sign. *Second part*: (1) Dorian transposed. (2) Freely composed. (3) M. 11, Infima Vox, note 2–m. 20, note 2, source has the flat on the fourth line. Concordance: Ame*H*, 1, pt. 2, pp. 252–254.

III. Ein ander Dancksagung
(1) Ionian transposed. (2) Possibly based on Helmbold's melody in Zahn*M*, no. 156. (3) M. 9, note 1–end, Infima Vox, the signature flat is on the third line in the source. Concordance: Kad*M*, appendix, p. 60.

IIII. Der 26. Psalm
(1) Ionian transposed. (2) Freely composed. (3) Incipit, Media Vox, in the source, the signature flat is in the top space. M. 26, note 3–m. 34, Media Vox, in the source, the signature flat is on the third line. M. 52, Infima Vox, note 1 is g in the source.

V. [Vater unser im Himmelreich]
(1) Dorian. (2) Based on a traditional chant melody, perhaps composed by Luther, in Zahn*M*, no. 2561, and in *WA* 35: 527.

VI. [Ein feste Burg]
(1) Ionian. (2) Based on a traditional chorale melody in Zahn*M*, no. 7377, and in *WA* 35: 518. (3) Concordances: Kad*M*, appendix, pp. 58–59, and Jöde*G*, pp. 119–120.

VII. [Kom Heiliger Geist]

(1) Ionian transposed. (2) Based on a traditional chorale melody in ZahnM, no. 7445a, and in WA 35: 510–512. (3) Concordance: AmeK, pp. 39–40.

VIII. [Nu bitten wir]

(1) Ionian transposed. (2) Based on a traditional chorale melody in ZahnM, no. 2029, and in WA 35: 510. (3) Concordances: MönkC, 1, pt. 2, pp. 106–107, and AmeK, pp. 44–45.

IX. [Gott sey gelobet]

(1) Mixolydian transposed. (2) Based on a traditional chorale melody in ZahnM, no. 8078, and in WA 35: 514–515. (3) Concordances: JödeG, pp. 20–22, and AmeK, pp. 91–92.

X. [Ein Kindelein so löbelich]

(1) Ionian transposed. (2) Based on the traditional chorale melody usually associated with the text "Der Tag der ist so freudenreich" ("Dies est leticie") in ZahnM, no. 7870. (3) Concordance: AmeH, 3, pt. 2, pp. 22–24. (1) Ionian transposed.

XI. [Gelobet seistu Jhesu Christ]

(1) Mixolydian. (2) Based on a traditional chorale melody in ZahnM, no. 1947, and in WA 35: 499. (3) Incipit, Infima Vox, source has C. M. 25, note 2–m. 35, note 2, Infima Vox, the clef is on the fifth line in the source. M. 35, note 3–end of piece, Infima Vox, clef is on the third line in the source. (3) Concordance: AmeK, pp. 6–7.

XII. [O Herr nim von mir]

(1) Ionian transposed. (2) Freely composed. (3) M. 10, note 1–m. 17, note 1, Infima Vox, source has the clef on the fourth line.

XIII. Von der Aufferstehung Christi

(1) Dorian. (2) Based on the traditional chorale melody derived from the melody for the Easter sequence, "Victimae paschali" (LU, p. 780) in ZahnM, no. 7012, and in WA 35: 506–507. (3) Incipit, Infima Vox, source has C. Concordance: AmeK, pp. 27–28.

XIIII. [Ach Gott von Himmel sich darein]

(1) Aeolian transposed. (2) Based on a traditional chorale melody in ZahnM, no. 4431, and in WA 35: 488–490. (3) Concordance: AmeK, pp. 100–101.

XV. [Erhalt uns Herr bey deinem Wort]

(1) Dorian transposed. (2) Based on a traditional chorale melody in ZahnM, no. 350, and in WA 35: 528. (3) Concordance: AmeH, 1, pt. 2, pp. 275–277.

XVI. [Verley uns frieden gnediglich]

(1) Dorian transposed. (2) Based on a traditional chorale melody in ZahnM, nos. 1945a and b, and in WA 35: 521. (3) Incipit, Suprema Vox, in the source, the flat is in the third space. Concordance: AmeH, 1, pt. 2, pp. 277–278.

XVII. [Gib unserm Fürsten und aller Oberkeit]

(1) Dorian transposed. (2) Based on a traditional chorale melody in ZahnM, no. 1945b. (3) M. 31, Media Vox, note 5 is a' in the source. Concordance: AmeH, 1, pt. 2, pp. 279–280.

XVIII. [Er rufft mich an]

(1) Ionian transposed. (2) Freely composed. (3) Concordance: AmeH, 2, pt. 1, pp. 22–23.

XIX. [Die Warheit ist gen Himel geflogen]

(1) Ionian transposed. (2) Freely composed.

XX. [Aus tieffer noth]

(1) Ionian transposed. (2) Freely composed. (3) Concordance: KadM, appendix, pp. 61–62.

XXI. Psalm. XC

(1) Ionian transposed. (2) Freely composed. (3) Incipit, Suprema Vox, source has C.

XXII. Dictum S. Augustini

(1) Aeolian transposed. (2) Freely composed. (3) Incipit, Infima Vox, source has the flat on the fourth line.

XXIII. Psalm. 119

(1) Ionian transposed. (2) Freely composed. (3) M. 26, Suprema Vox, note 3 is g' in the source. M. 34, Infima Vox, here the source is smudged, with only the note stems faintly visible; the pitches and the rhythms of this measure are editorial conjecture.

XXIIII. [Si mundus hic demonibus]

(1) Dorian. (2) Freely composed. (3) M. 45, Media Vox, note 3 is b' in the source. M. 48, Media Vox, source lacks the semibreve-rest. M. 55, Media Vox, a *punctus additionis* is inserted between notes 1 and 2 in the source.

Acknowledgments

Special thanks are herewith tendered to Professor Louise Cuyler for her guidance in my study of Le Maistre's music, to Professor Patricia Marquardt for her translations of Le Maistre's Latin prefaces to the *Catechesis* and *Gesenge*, and to the Bayerische Staatsbibliothek, the British Library, and the Deutsches Musikgeschichtliches Archiv for providing the microfilms of Le Maistre's compositions.

July 1981

Donald Gresch
Milwaukee, Wisconsin

Notes

1. ". . . unnd sobald wir einen newen Capellnmeyster neben etlichenn gesellen unnd knaben aus Niderlanden ann die Hannd bracht." Moritz Fürstenau, "Churfürstliche Sechsische Canntoreiordnung," *Monatshefte für Musikgeschichte* 9 (1887): 236.

2. "Et quo minus mihi studio Musices à Iuuentute addicto."

3. For example, Ernst Gerber erroneously concluded that before his appointment in Dresden, Le Maistre held the position of choirmaster at the cathedral in Milan. See Ernst Ludwig Gerber, *Neues historisch-biographisches Lexikon der Tonkünstler* (Leipzig: A. Kühnel, 1812–1813), 3: cols. 388–389. Gerber's supposition was successfully contested by Franz Haberl in his article "Matthias Hermann Werrecorensis. Eine bibliographische-kritische Studie," *Monatshefte für Musikgeschichte* 3 (1871): 197–200.

4. Adolf Sandberger, *Beiträge zur Geschichte der bayerischen Hofkapelle unter Orlando di Lasso* (Leipzig: Breitkopf und Härtel, 1894), 1: 50–53.

5. Julius Maier, *Die musikalischen Handschriften der K. Hof- und Staatsbibliothek in München* (Munich: Palm'schen Hofbuchhandlung, 1897), no. 66.

6. A facsimile of this letter appears in L. Otto Kade, *Mattheus Le Maistre* (Mainz: B. Schott's Söhne, 1862), facing p. viii.

7. Fürstenau, "Churfürstliche Sechsische Canntoreiordnung," pp. 235–246.

8. Moritz Fürstenau, "Zwei Aktenstücke, den Kurfürstlichen Sächsischen Kapellmeister Mattheus Le Maistre betreffend," *Monatshefte für Musikgeschichte* 10 (1878): 60–61.

9. Ibid., pp. 61–63.

10. "ILLVSTRISSIMI PRINCIPIS, DOMINI D. AVGVSTI, ELECTORIS, ET ARCHIMARSCALCI S. Romani imperij, Saxoniæ Ducis &c. Domini mei clementiss. &c. Filio, D. D. Alexandro &c. S. S.

Magna laus est, Deo grata, & ad omnem posteritatem propaganda, esse Principes Dei beneficio adhuc in hac ærumnosa mundi senecta superstites, qui gloriam Dei sine fuco, & ficto zelo, quærere student. Nec iam de alijs loquor, ne uidear mihi iudicium de rebus supra meum captum positis tribuere. De te, Inclyte Alexander, uerba facio, qui pietate insigni parentum tuorum merito moueris ad studium acre pietatis iam à teneris tuis, quod dici solet, unguiculis. Deo patri Domini nostri Iesu Christi sit laus & gloria, qui sub patre tuo Domino meo clementissimo ueram, et incorruptam doctrinam legis et Euangelij in Misnia adhuc conseruat contra omnes insultus, & fucos diabolorum, & hominum ΤΩΝ ΑΠΟΠΛΗΚΤΩΝ. Hunc quoque ardentibus uotis oramus, ut deinceps in hac regione colligat sibi agmen docentium, & discentium ueram doctrinam legis & Euangelij.

Vt autem ad rem, de quacum serenitate tua iam agendum esse mihi persuadeo, breuibus ueniam, offero hic ΚΑΤΗΧΗΣΙΜ Celsitudinis tuæ ætati conuenientem, hoc est, forma & serie succincta & uera scriptam, numerisque nostris musicis, qui teneræ ætati sunt conuenientissimi, inclusam. Ad hanc me primum (nam & hoc mihi reticendum non est) cohortando adegit M. Nicolaus Selneccerus, ut scilicet pueri in choro nostro musico tali propemodum forma uterentur. Et cum bonis uiris non displicere nostrum hoc studium intelligerem, monitu Selnecceri & aliorum, tandem passus sum edi in lucem, non quod quiddam arte peculiari scriptum proferrem, qui scio numeros hos pueriles esse, sed pietatis causa, quæ tuæ, ut dixi, Celsitudini cordi est. Nec dubito Celsitudinem tuam boni & æqui probaturam esse meum officium. Et spero candidos iudices mihi æquos fore, qui causam mei consilij cognoscent. De alijs non loquendum esse censeo. Iudicio abundet quilibet suo. Tuam Celsitudinem Deo commendo, qui uniuersum stemma Celsitudinis tuæ incolume, & superstes conseruet, Amen.
Tuæ Celsitudini deditiss. Matthæus le Meistre, Sacelli Magister."

11. "ILLVSTRISSIMO PRINCIPI, AC DOMINO, DOMINO CHRISTIANO DVCI SAXONIÆ, SERENISSIMI ET POtentissimi Principis Electoris Augusti &c. Filio, Landgrauio Thuringiæ & Marchioni Misniæ, Domino suo Clementissimo, S. P. D.

CUM IN ECCLESIA DEI Illustrissime Princeps, Domine Clementissime, in nomine Indiuiduæ Trinitatis, sacro sanctum officium & conciones Diuinæ, Cancionibus & precationibus quidem deuotissimis, pro more Apostolorum, vt in Actis legimus, ordiri vsitatum sit. Deus enim propterea hominibus veram numerorum & Harmoniæ ita noticiam indidit, Doctrinam cœelestem, laudesque diuinas in celebrationem sui nominis, & nostram salutem comprehendi voluit: vt verba sacra & sanctæ Doctrinæ altius animos auditorum penetrent, pietatisquè ardentiores motus in cordibus fidelium accendant, vti odarum genera, viri Moysis, Iosuæ, Dauidis, Asaph, Salomonis, Esaiæ & Ieremiæ &c. ostendunt.

Hoc nostro vltimo, & propter Dei expressum verbum, aureo sæculo, in omnibus linguis talia, quæ animabus nostris (vt. D. Basilius refert) natura coniuncta, in Ecclesiarum vsum creuisse, sit altissimo Deo laus sempiterna, & gloria in perpetuum.

Nam D. Lutherus Orpheus Germanicus laudatæ memoriæ, Psalmos precipuos Dauidis hominum affectibus Idoneos, suis Harmonijs ita eneruose rithmis donauit, vt omnes Nationes quibus nostra lingua nota est, eaquè delectantur id celebrent & commendent: Cuius pietatem, animiquè feruorem & nos quidem sanctè probamus, & non immerito imitamur.

Nam Psalmos canere, est munus Angelicum, cœeleste Politeuma & spirituale Thimiama.

Et quo minus mihi studio Musices à Iuuentute addicto, meæque Familiæ consolationibus deessem, & ægritudinis meæ torturam aliquo modo minuerem, Tricinia hæc composui, & sic Patrueli Dauidis, Christo meo, Salutari nostro, vnico animarum nostrarum Redemptori nouum canticum cecini: Et Podagra diu multumque vexatus melius excogitare non potui, nec debui.

Quo autem mihi aliquem eligam, cui studium meum Musices minus displiceat & non aspernetur, Illustrissime Princeps, Domine Mecœnas Clementissime, præter vestram Ill: Celsitudinem, scio neminem, peritis Musicis in hoc gratificari nequeo: Sed Studiosis Iuuenibus, qui exercicij loco, & pro gratiarum actione, ante & post Mensam, mecum canere desiderant, ijs inseruio.

Et ne de grauissimo ingratitudinis vicio accusari possim, (nam me totum Illustrissimæ Domui Saxoniæ debeo) Vestræ Ill: Cels. hunc tenuem & paruum laborem nuncupo & dedico: quem Vest: Ilust: Cels: à me benignè accipere dignetur, quod maximopere peto & flagito. Quia virum decet, vt Sophocles docet, meminisse, si quid gratum ei accidit: Gratia enim semper gignit gratiam, cui vero accepti beneficij memoria effluit, nunque hic erit generosus vir. Et Cicero asserit, Etenim iudices, cum me virtutibus omnibus affectum esse cupiam, tum nihil est quod malim, quam me & gratum esse & videri.

Deo Trino & uni vestram Illust: Celsitudinem & vniuersam Saxoniæ Domum commendo. Dabantur Calendis Ianuarij, Anno à nato Christo M. D. LXXVII.

Vest: Illust: Cel: Subiectissimus Matth: le Maistre Senior Capellæ Magister.''

12. Kade, *Mattheus Le Maistre*, p. 42.

13. Martin Luther, *D. Martin Luthers Werke* (Weimar: Hermann Böhlaus Nachfolger, 1910), 30, pt. 1, pp. 241–402. Its form does approximate a Latin version made for young schoolboys by Justus Jonas and published in Wittenberg in 1539. Jonas's version includes the five principal parts with somewhat abbreviated interpretive glosses, but it does not include either of the two table prayers included by Le Maistre in the *Catechesis*. Many of the details of the text of Jonas's version do not correspond to those of Le Maistre's. See *D. Martin Luthers Werke*, 30, pt. 1, pp. 403-411.

14. ''. . . Hodie quantum prosint Ecclesiæ cantilenæ à D. M. Luthero & alijs pijs (quorum memoria sit in benedictione) compositæ, dictu haud facilè est, cum manifestum sit, & summam doctrinæ Christianæ in his contineri, & iuuentutem rudeque vulgus istiusmodi Melodijs ad veram religionem facilius traduci posse. Quam ob causam & Reuerendus vir D. Lutherus Musicæ proximum dignitatis locum post Theologiam attribuit, quod ministra huius esset, & ad conseruandam doctrinæ puritatem non parum conferret.''

15. Kade, *Mattheus Le Maistre*, p. 44. ''Fast allen Tonsätzen hat Le Maistre, so weit es zu verfolgen mir möglich gewesen ist, den aus der katholischen Kirche stammenden, später auch zum grossen Theil in die protestantische übergegangenen Gregorianischen Cantus firmus zu Grunde gelegt.''

16. Luther, *D. Martin Luthers Werke*, 35: 495.

17. The occasional melodic similarities between Le Maistre's setting of the first part of *Catechesis* no. VII, the ''Gratiarum Actio'' (''Confitemi Domino''), and the Alleluia verse from the *Mass of the Paschal Vigil* (*Liber Usualis* [Tournai: Desclée & Soc., 1962], p. 776ii) are neither consistent nor obvious enough to suggest that Le Maistre consciously regarded the chant as a model for his polyphonic setting of this prayer.

18. ''. . . auch von ihm selbst Corrigiert, und in Druck geordnet.''

19. Kade, *Mattheus Le Maistre*, pp. 84–85.

20. For Zarlino's rules, see Oliver Strunk, *Source Readings in Music History* (New York: W. W. Norton, 1950), pp. 259–261.

Text Sources and Translations

Translations of Latin and German scriptural texts are taken verbatim from the King James version of the Bible. All other Latin and German texts, whether originally prose or poetry, are translated here into English prose. These translations are the work of the editor, who, in their preparation, freely consulted the standard translations of many of these popular religious song texts. The translation of each text is preceded by the name of the original author or the source of the original text, together with references to other sources in which the complete or authoritative version of the text may be found. (See the List of Abbreviations in the Appendix on p. xxiii for these references.)

The Catechism

I. The Ten Commandments

Based on Exod. 20:2–17 and Deut. 5:6–21. *WA*, 30, pt. 1, pp. 283–291, 403–405.

The Lord's Ten Commandments.
I am the Lord thy God.
Thou shalt have no other gods before me.
Thou shalt not take the name of the Lord thy God in vain; for the Lord will not hold him guiltless that taketh his name in vain.
Remember the sabbath day, to keep it holy.
Honor thy father and thy mother: that thy days may be long upon the land which the Lord thy God giveth thee.
Thou shalt not kill.
Thou shalt not commit adultery.
Thou shalt not steal.
Thou shalt not bear false witness against thy neighbor.
Thou shalt not covet thy neighbor's house, thou shalt not covet thy neighbor's wife, nor his manservant, nor his maidservant, nor his ox, nor his ass, nor anything that is thy neighbor's.

II. The Apostle's Creed

WA, 30, pt. 1, pp. 292–299, 406–407.

I believe in God the Father almighty, maker of heaven and earth.
And in Jesus Christ his only son, our Lord; who was conceived by the Holy Ghost, born of the virgin Mary, suffered under Pontius Pilate, was crucified, dead and buried. He descended into hell. The third day he arose again from the dead. He ascended into heaven, and sitteth on the right hand of God the Father almighty, from whence he shall come to judge the quick and the dead.
I believe in the Holy Spirit, the holy Christian church, the communion of saints, the forgiveness of sins, the resurrection of the body, and life everlasting. Amen.

III. The Lord's Prayer

Matt. 6:9–13. *WA*, 30, pt. 1, pp. 298–309, 407–409.

Our Father, which art in heaven, hallowed be thy name.
Thy kingdom come. Thy will be done on earth, as it is in heaven.
Give us this day our daily bread.
And forgive us our debts, as we forgive our debtors.
And lead us not into temptation, but deliver us from evil.

IIII. On Baptism

Matt. 28:19 and Mark 16:16. *WA*, 30, pt. 1, pp. 308–313, 409–410.

Go ye therefore, and teach all nations, baptizing them in the name of the Father, and of the Son, and of the Holy Ghost.
He that believeth and is baptized shall be saved; but he that believeth not shall be damned.

V. On the Lord's Supper

Based on Matt. 26:26–28, Mark 14:22–24, Luke 22:19–20, and 1 Cor. 11:23–25. *WA*, 30, pt. 1, pp. 314–319, 411.

Our Lord Jesus Christ, the same night in which he was betrayed, took bread.
And when he had given thanks, he broke it, and said, "Take, eat, this is my body which is given for you; this do in remembrance of me."
After the same manner and after he had supped he took the cup, and when he had given thanks he gave it to them, saying, "Drink ye all of it, for this cup is the new testament in my blood, which is shed for you for the remission of sins; this do as oft as ye drink it in remembrance of me."

VI. Table Blessing

First part—Ps. 145:15–16. *WA*, 30, pt. 1, pp. 322–325. Second part—a reworking of the versicle "Benedic Domini nos" (*BM*, 1:259). *WA*, 30, pt. 1, pp. 324–325.

The eyes of all wait upon thee; and thou givest them their meat in due season.

Thou openest thine hand, and satisfiest the desire of every living thing.

Lord God, heavenly Father, bless us and these thy gifts, which we receive from thy bountiful goodness, through Jesus Christ our Lord. Amen.

VII. Giving Thanks

First part—Ps. 136:1 and 147:9–11. *WA*, 30, pt. 1, pp. 324–327. Second part—a reworked version of the versicle "Agimus tibi gratias" (*BM*, 1:259–260). *WA*, 30, pt. 1, pp. 326–327.

O give thanks unto the Lord; for he is good: for his mercy endureth for ever.

He giveth to the beast his food, and to the young ravens which cry.

He delighteth not in the strength of the horse, and taketh not pleasure in the legs of a man.

The Lord taketh pleasure in them that fear him, in those that hope in his mercy.

We thank thee, Lord God our Father, for thy gracious gifts, through Jesus Christ our Lord, who livest and reignest for ever. Amen.

The Songs

I. The Table Blessing

First part—Ps. 145:15–16. *WA*, 30, pt. 1, pp 322–325. Second part—Matt. 6:9–13. Third part—a reworking and German translation of the versicle "Benedic Domini nos" (*BM*, 1:259). *WA*, 30, pt. 1, pp. 324–325.

The eyes of all wait upon thee; and thou givest them their meat in due season.

Thou openest thine hand, and satisfiest the desire of every living thing.

Our Father which art in heaven, hallowed be thy name.

Thy kingdom come. Thy will be done in earth as it is in heaven.

Give us this day our daily bread.

And forgive us our debts, as we forgive our debtors.

Lord God, heavenly Father, bless us and these thy gifts, which we receive from thy bountiful goodness, through Jesus Christ our Lord. Amen.

II. Giving Thanks

First part—Ps. 136:1 and 147:9–11. *WA*, 30, pt. 1, pp. 324–327. Second part—a German translation and reworking of the versicle "Agimus tibi gratias" (*BM*, 1:259–260). *WA*, 30, pt. 1, pp. 326–327.

O give thanks unto the Lord; for he is good; for his mercy endureth forever.

He giveth to the beast his food, and to the young ravens which cry.

He delighteth not in the strength of the horse, he taketh not pleasure in the legs of a man.

The Lord taketh pleasure in them that fear him, in those that hope in his mercy.

We thank thee, Lord God our Father, for thy gracious gifts, through Jesus Christ our Lord, who livest and reignest for ever. Amen.

III. Another Thanksgiving

Ludwig Helmbold. *WackerK*, 4:647.

We now thank the Lord,
as is right and proper,
for the gifts
which we have received.

For our body, soul, and life
he alone has given us,
and to preserve them
he will not spare his mercy.

A physician is given us,
which is life itself;
Christ, who died for us,
has bought our salvation.

His cross, passion and death
prevent our destruction;
the Holy Spirit, through faith,
teaches us to trust in them.

Preserve us in truth;
grant us always the freedom
to praise thy name
through Jesus Christ. Amen.

IIII. The 26th Psalm

Anonymous paraphrase of Ps. 26. The unique source is Le Maistre's *Gesenge*.

Lord, now rightly judge thy servant, for my uprightness is known to thee;

I trust in thee, do not forsake me, for I am diligent.

I shall not falter, I am pledged not to waver from thy word;

Test me, and examine me, and guide all my thoughts.

Purify my heart, spare me not, and therewith purify
my bowels;
For in love I yield myself to thee; thy kindness is before my eyes.
And I walk upright, in simple truth; protect me
from worthless men;
Those who are vain I speedily shun, and I do not sit
at their side.

The assembly of evildoers I guard against, and de-
spise them in my heart;
Because thou art gracious, in innocence I now wash
my hands.
And keep me, Lord, so I may thank thee, always
near thy altar;
Where thou art praised, thy word is taught, and thy
wondrous deeds proclaimed.

Therefore I love, in faithful constancy, thy word according to thy will;
Thy house is the place wherein thy blessed word is
manifest,
Where thy glory, holy and noble, itself inhabits the
city;
For thy glory, I fervently pray, that thou wilt par-
don me.

And my soul, for my salvation, preserve now in
mercy;
Take it not up [with those] in the path [of sin]; govern me at all times.
How guilty, in malice, is the hoard of sinners beyond measure;
Snatch my life from danger, and never forsake me.

And how they, esteemed everywhere, have be-
come bloodthirsty;
Do not punish me, be merciful to me, and for thy
sake make me whole.
Root out and remove those evil thoughts that pre-
sume to be malicious;
Those who take bribes, malicious deceivers, have I
zealously disavowed.

Then for thy sake I acknowledge everywhere my innocence and my actions;
Redeem me, be merciful to me, my foot is steadfast
in its course.
Thou goest from hence, for which, Lord, I will
praise thee wholly;
Whenever they, the pious congregation, will speak
of thy word and thy law.

V. [Our Father in heaven]

Martin Luther's hymn based on the first lines of the
Lord's Prayer (Matt. 6:9–13). *WA*, 35:463–465.

Our Father in heaven,
who bids us all
to dwell as brothers, and to call upon thee
and will have us pray to thee:
Teach us to pray not only with our lips,
help us to pray from our inmost heart.

VI. [Our God is a stronghold sure]

Martin Luther's paraphrase of Ps. 46. *WA*, 35:
455–457.

Our God is a stronghold sure,
a trusty weapon and defense.
He freely helps us in every need,
that befalls us here.
The old evil foe,
earnestly he sets against us
his great power and cunning;
with terror as his armor,
his equal does not exist on earth.

VII. [Come, Holy Spirit]

Martin Luther, based on the antiphon "Veni sancte
spiritus" (*LU*, pp. 1837-1838). *WA*, 35:448–449.

Come, Holy Spirit, Lord God,
pour out thy gracious mercies
on each believer's heart, mind, and soul,
and kindle thy fervent love in them.
O Lord, through thy brilliant radiance
in faith thou hast assembled
men of all tongues;
for which, Lord, thy praise is sung.
Alleluia.

VIII. [We now pray the Holy Spirit]

Martin Luther. *WA*, 35:447–448.

We now pray the Holy Spirit
especially for true faith,
that he protect us at our end,
when we travel from this misery toward our home.
Lord have mercy.

IX. [God be praised]

Martin Luther. *WA*, 35:452–453.

God be praised and blessed,
who has nourished even us
with his body and blood;
give us that, Lord God, for our salvation.
Lord have mercy.

Lord, through thy holy body,
born of thy mother, Mary,
and thy holy blood,
help us, Lord, out of all misery.
Lord have mercy.

X. [A child so worthy]

Anonymous. Wacker*K*, 3:520–521.

A child so worthy
is born today
of a virgin pure
for the consolation of poor folk.
Had the child not been born,
then would we be lost forever;
our salvation is our everything.
Oh, sweet Jesus Christ,
born a man,
protect us from the infernal.

XI. [Praise to thee, Jesus Christ]

Martin Luther. *WA*, 35:434–435.

Praise to thee, Jesus Christ,
who was truly born a man
by a virgin;
whereof the angel host rejoices.
Lord have mercy.

XII. [O Lord, purge from me]

Anonymous. The unique source is Le Maistre's *Ge-senge.*

O Lord, purge from me
what turns me from thee;
O Lord, give to me
what turns me to thee;
O Lord, take me away from myself
and give me wholly to thee.

XIII. On Christ's Resurrection

Martin Luther's reworking of the text of the ancient hymn "Christ ist erstranden." *WA*, 35:443–445.

Christ lay in the bonds of death
sacrificed for our sins,
but he has arisen
and brought us life;
whereof we shall rejoice,
praise God and be thankful
and sing alleluia.
Alleluia.

XIIII. [O Lord, look down]

Martin Luther's paraphrase of Ps. 12. *WA*, 35:415–417.

O Lord, look down from heaven
and be merciful;
how few are thy saints,
we poor faithful are forsaken.
Thy word is despised,
faith is completely extinguished
among the children of men.

XV. [Keep us, Lord, steadfast]

Anonymous reworking of a chorale text ("Ein Kinderlied, zu singen, wider die zween Ertzfeinde Christi und seiner heiligen Kirchen, den Bapst und Türcken, etc.") originally by Martin Luther. Luther's version in *WA*, 35:467–468.

Keep us, Lord, steadfast in Thy word
and foil the devil's deceit and threat;
through true doctrine in all the world
grant us peace now and hereafter.

XVI. [Kindly grant us peace]

Martin Luther's paraphrase of the *Antiphona pro pace* (*LU*, pp. 1867–1868). *WA*, 35:458.

Kindly grant us peace,
Lord God, in our time;
there is none other,
who can fight for us,
except thee, our God, alone.

XVII. [Grant to our princes]

Anonymous reworking of 1 Tim. 2:2.

Grant to our princes, and all officials, peace and a good rule; that we, under them, may lead a quiet and peaceful life in all godliness and honesty. Amen.

XVIII. [He shall call upon me]

Ps. 91:15–16 (Vulgate).

He shall call upon me, and I will answer him: I will be with him in trouble; I will deliver him, and honor him.
With long life will I satisfy him, and show him my salvation.

XIX. [Truth has blown to the winds]

Anonymous. The unique source is Le Maistre's *Ge-senge.*

Truth has blown to the winds,
honesty has escaped across the sea;
righteousness is driven out,
heresy remains in the world.

XX. [From depths of woe]

Anonymous, the beginning based on Ps. 130:1–2.

From depths of woe, o faithful God,
I cry to thee, be merciful to me;
turn thy ear toward me,
and forgive my sins, and abide with me.
Then I will speak thanks to thee,
for thy goodness, and thy mercy,
and praise thee in eternity. Amen.

XXI. Psalm. XC

Ps. 90:15–16 (Vulgate).

He shall call upon me, and I will answer him: I will be with him in trouble; I will deliver him, and honor him.
With long life will I satisfy him, and show him my salvation.

XXII. A saying of St. Augustine

Attributed to St. Augustine.

Disquieted I am, but not confounded, because I remember the wounds of Christ.

XXIII. Psalm 119

First part—Ps. 119:1. Second part—source of "Cui sit gloria, . . ." is unidentified.

In my distress I cried unto the Lord, and he heard me.
To Him be praise and thanksgiving for ever, world without end. Amen.

XXIIII. [Though devils in this world]

Anonymous Latin translation of the third strophe, "Und wenn die welt voll Teuffel wer," of Luther's chorale "Ein feste burg." The original German version is in *WA*, 35:456–457.

Though devils in this world
abound as vermin,
we are not fearful;
we will conquer in the end.
The arrogant worldly prince,
snarl and rage though he will;
the worthless imp cannot harm
with either word or deed.

Appendix

List of Abbreviations

AmeH   Ameln, K.; Mahrenholz, W.; and Thomas, W., eds. *Handbuch der deutschen evangelischen Kirchenmusik.* 3 vols. Göttingen: Vandenhoeck und Ruprecht, 1933–1940.

AmeK   Ameln, K., ed. *Luthers Kirchenlieder in Tonsätzen seiner Zeit.* Kassel: Bärenreiter-Verlag, 1934.

BM   *Brevarium Monasticum.* 2 vols. Bruges: Desclée, 1931.

FaMGG   Farmer, H. G., "Pater noster." In *Die Musik in Geschichte und Gegenwart*, vol. 10, edited by Friedrich Blume. Bärenreiter-Verlag, 1962.

GötzC   Götz, R., ed. *Chorgesangbuch. Geistliche Gesänge für ein bis fünf Stimmen.* Kassel: Bärenreiter-Verlag, 1969.

JödeG   Jöde, F., ed. *Geistliche Lieder und Gesänge für gleiche Stimmen.* Das Chorbuch für Musikanten, vol. 5. Wolfenbüttel: G. Kallmeyer, 1930.

KadM   Kade, L. O. *Mattheus Le Maistre.* Mainz: B. Schott's Söhne, 1862.

LU   *Liber Usualis.* Tournai: Desclée, 1961.

MaldR   Maldeghem, R. van, ed. *Trésor Musical. Musique religieuse.* 29 vols. 1865–1893. Reprint. Vaduz, Liechtenstein: Kraus, 1965.

MönkeC   Mönkemeyer, H., ed. *Antiqua Chorbuch.* 2 vols. Mainz: B. Schott's Söhne, 1951–1952.

WA   [Weimarer Ausgabe] *D. Martin Luthers Werke: Kritische Gesamtausgabe.* Weimar: Hermann Böhlaus Nachfolger, 1883– .

WackerK   Wackernagel, P. *Das deutsche Kirchenlied von den ältesten Zeiten bis zum Anfang des XVII. Jahrhunderts.* 5 vols. Leipzig: B. G. Teubner, 1863–1877.

ZahnM   Zahn, J. *Die Melodien der Deutschen Evangelischen Kirchenlieder.* 6 vols. 1889–1893. Reprint, Hildesheim: Georg Ohlms Verlagsbuchhandlung, 1963.

Plate I. Title page, *Catechesis numeris musicis inclusa*, Mattheus Le Maistre,
first edition, Nuremberg, 1559.
(By permission of The British Library)

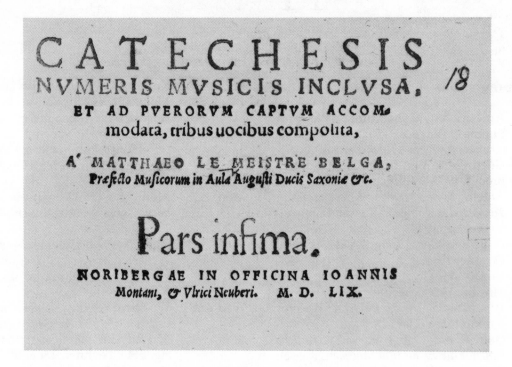

Plate II. Pars Infima, first page of music, *Catechesis numeris musicis inclusa*,
Mattheus Le Maistre, first edition, Nuremberg, 1559.
(By permission of The British Library)

CATECHESIS NUMERIS MUSICIS INCLUSA

I. Decem Praecepta Dei

[Unison]

De- cem prae- ce- pta_ De- i.

Primus Discantus

E- go sum Do- mi- nus De-

Secundus Discantus

E- go sum Do- mi- nus

Pars Infima

E- go sum Do- mi- nus De-

-us tu- - us, tu- - us. Non ha- be- bis De- os

De- us tu- - us. _____ Non ha- be- bis De- os

- us tu- us. _____ Non ha- be- bis De- os

a- li- e- nos co- ram me. Non as- su- mes no- men Do- mi-

a- li- e- nos co- ram me. Non as- su- mes no- men Do- mi-

a- li- e- nos co- ram me. Non as- su- mes no- men Do- mi-

-ni De- i tu- i in va- num. Ne- que e- nim in- son-

-ni De- i tu- i in va- num. Ne- que e- nim in- son-

-ni De- i tu- i in va- num. Ne- que e- nim in- son-

4

nec an- cil- lam, nec iu- men- tum, nec om- ni- a quae
nec an- cil- lam, nec iu- men- tum, nec om- ni- a quae
nec an- cil- lam, nec iu- men- tum, nec om- ni- a quae

il- li- us sunt.
il- li- us sunt, il- li- us sunt.
il- li- us sunt.

II. Symbolum Apostolorum

Primus Discantus

Cre- do in u- num De- um pa- trem om-

Secundus Discantus

Cre- do in u- num De- um pa- trem om-

Pars Infima

Cre- do in u- num De- um pa- trem om-

-ni- po- ten- tem fa- cto- rem coe- li et ter- rae.
-ni- po- ten- tem fa- cto- rem coe- li et ter- rae.
-ni- po- ten- tem fa- cto- rem coe- li et ter- rae.

Et in Ie- sum Chri- stum, [Ie- sum Chri- stum] fi- li- um

Et in Ie- sum Chri- stum, Ie- - sum Chri- stum fi- li- um

Et in Ie- sum Chri- stum, [Ie- - sum Chri- stum] fi- li- um

e- ius u- ni- cum Do- mi- num no- - stum, qui con-

e- ius u- ni- cum Do- mi- num no- - strum, qui con-

e- ius u- ni- cum Do- mi- num___ no- strum, qui con-

-ce- ptus est de spi- ri- tu san- cto, na- tus ex Ma- ri- a

-ce- ptus est de spi- ri- tu san- cto, na- tus ex Ma- ri- a

-ce- ptus est de spi- ri- tu san- cto, na- tus ex Ma- ri- a

vir- gi- ne, pas- sus sub Pon- ti- o___ Pi- la-

vir- gi- ne, pas- sus sub Pon- ti- o Pi- - la-

vir- gi- ne, pas- sus sub Pon- ti- o Pi- - la-

-to, Cru- ci- fi- xus mor- tu- us et se- pul- tus, de- scen-

-to, Cru- ci- fi- xus mor- tu- us et se- pul- tus, de- scen-

-to, Cru- ci- fi- xus mor- tu- us et se- pul- tus, de- scen-

III. Oratio Dominica
4. voc.

IIII. De Baptismo

V. De Coena Domini

VI. Benedictio Mensae

Oculi. Benedicte. Confitemini. Gratias.
Haec ex Discanti voce certis fugis canenda sunt.

VII. Gratiarum Actio
Canon in subdiapente.

21

SCHÖNE UND AUSERLESENE
DEUDSCHE UND LATEINISCHE GEISTLICHE GESENGE

I. Das Benedicite

32

nicht in ver- su- chung, Son- dern er- lö- se— uns, son-

ver- su- chung, Son- dern er- lö- se

in ver- su- chung, Son- dern er- lö-

-dern er- lö- se uns von dem u- bel, A- men.

uns von dem u- bel, A- men.

se uns von dem u- bel, A- men.

Her- re Gott Him- li- scher Va- ter, ge-

Her- re Gott Him- li- scher Va- ter,

Her- re Gott Him- li- scher Va- ter, ge- seg- ne

-seg- ne uns und die- se dei- ne ga- ben,

ge- seg- ne uns und die- se dei- ne ga- ben, die

uns und die- se dei- ne ga- ben, die

II. Das Gratias

* The "Vater unser" from the second section of number I, "Das Benedicite," should be sung here.

36

III. Ein ander Dancksagung

Nu last uns Gott den Herren, Dancksagen und in ehren,
  Von wegen seiner gaben, die wir empfangen haben.

Den Leib, die Seel das Leben, Hat er allein uns geben,
  Denselben zubewaren, Thut er sein güte nicht sparen.

Ein Artzt ist uns gegeben, derselbe ist das leben,
  Christus für uns gestorben, hat uns das heyl erworben.

Sein Kreutz, sein leiden, sein Nachtmal, das dienet wider den unfall,
  Der heilige Geist im glauben, lehrt uns fest darauff bawen.

Erhalt uns in der warheit, du ewigliche freyheit,
  Zum preis deins Göttlichen namens, Durch Jhesum Christum, Amen.

IIII. Der 26. Psalm

Herr deinem Knecht, schaff jtzund recht, Mein unschuldt sey dir wissendt,
Ich hoff auff dich, verlas mich nicht, darumb bin ich geflissen.
Wil gleiten nicht, dir sein verpflicht, von deinem Wort nicht wancken,
Des prüfe mich, versuch wie ich, anstell all mein gedancken.

Leuter mein Hertz, wend traurens schmertz, Purgier darzu mein Nieren,
Denn ich in lieb, mich dich ergieb, dein gut für augen fur.
Und wandel recht, in warheit schlecht, hüte mich für falschen Leuten,
Die eitel sind, meid ich geschwind, sitz nicht an ihre seidten.

Der losen schar, nim ich auch war, von hertzen sie verhasse,
Fur deine huld, ich mein unschuld, allhie mein hende wassche.
Und halt mich Herr, zu dancken mehr, bey dem Altar besunder,
Da man dich rümbt, dein Wort vornimpt, verkündt all deine wunder.

Daher ich lieb, in stetter jeb, die Lehr nach deinem willen,
Dein haus das ort, der gnaden Wort, dieselbe zu erfüllen.
Da deine Ehr, heilig und Hehr, Selbst ist, die stedt bewohnet,
Zu deinem Preis, bitt ich mit fleis, wolst du meiner verschonen.

Und meine Seel, zu meinem heil, in gnaden hie erhalte,
Raff sie nicht auff, in solchem lauff, mein wollest allzeit walten.
Wie hat verschuld, in ungedult, der Sünder hauff onmassen,
Mein leben zwar, reis aus gefahr, thue mich keines weges verlassen.

Und wie auch die, verdient allhie, blutdurstig seind gewesen,
Nicht straffe mich, erbarm dich, für dir las mir genesen.
Reut aus nim hin, welch böser sinn, zu argen ist gewehnet,
Nemen geschenck, tückischer renck, drücklich habens vorneinet.

Denn ich für dir, bekenn allheir, die unschuld und mein handel,
Erlöse mich, sey mir gnedig. Richtig mein fus in wandel,
Gehet daher, dafur ich Herr, dich loben wil versamlet,
Wenn die wird sein, die from Gemein, dein Wort und lehre handelt.

V. [Vater unser im Himmelreich]

20
uns han,] Gib das nicht bet al- - lein
uns han,] Gib das nicht bet al- lein der mund, al- lein
das be- ten von uns han,] Gib das nicht bet al-
25
der mund, [Gib das nicht bet al- lein
der mund, [Gib das nicht bet al- lein
-lein der mund, [Gib das nicht bet al- lein der mund,
30
der mund,] Hilff das es geh von her- tzen
der mund,] Hilff das es geh von her- - tzen
al- lein der mund,] Hilff das es geh von her- tzen grund, Hilff
35
grund, [Hilff das es geh von her- - - tzen grund.]
grund, [von her- tzen grund,] Hilff das es geh von her- tzen grund.
das es geh von her- tzen grund, [Hilff das es geh von her- tzen grund.]

VI. [Ein feste Burg]

VII. [Kom Heiliger Geist]

VIII. [Nu bitten wir]

50

IX. [Gott sey gelobet]

__ mit sei- nem blu- - te,] das gib uns ____ Herr Gott zu gu-

gib uns Herr Gott zu gu- - te, Ky- ri- e- lei-

-sche und mit sei- nem blu- te,] das gib uns Herr Gott zu

-te, Ky- ri- e- lei- - son, [Ky- ri- e- lei- son.]

-son, [Ky- ri- e- lei- - son, Ky- ri- e- lei- - son. ____]

gu- te, Ky- ri- e- lei- - son, [Ky- ri- e- lei- son.]

Herr durch dei- nen hei- li- gen Leich- nam, der

Herr durch dei- nen hei- li- gen Leich- nam, der

Herr durch dei- nen hei- li- gen Leich- nam, der __

von dei- - ner Mut- ter Ma- ri- - a kam, und

von dei- ner ____ Mut- ter ____ Ma- ri- a __ kam, und das

__ von dei- - ner Mut- - ter ____ Ma- ri- - a

54

X. [Ein Kindelein so löbelich]

XI. [Gelobet seistu Jhesu Christ]

58

XII. [O Herr nim von mir]

XIII. Von der Aufferstehung Christi

XIIII. [Ach Gott von Himmel sich darein]

66

XV. [Erhalt uns Herr bey deinem Wort]

XVI. [Verley uns frieden gnediglich]

70

XVII. [Gib unserm Fürsten und aller Oberkeit]

XVIII. [Er rufft mich an]

- ten, Ich bin bey ihm in der noth, [Ich bin bey ihm in der

-ret-   ten, Ich bin bey ihm in der noth, [Ich bin bey ihm in der

-ret-   ten,] Ich bin bey ihm in der noth, [Ich bin bey ihm in der

noth,]   Ich _____ wil ihn her- aus- reis- sen, [her- aus-reis-

noth,] Ich wil _____ ihn her- aus- reis-   sen, [her- aus-reis-

noth,] Ich wil ihn her- aus- reis-   sen, her- aus-

- sen,]   und   zu eh- ren ma-

-    sen,] und _____ zu eh- ren ma-   chen, [und _____ zu eh- ren

-reis-   sen,   und   zu eh- ren ma-   chen, [und   zu

- chen, [und   zu eh- ren ma-   chen,]   Ich

ma-   -   chen,   und zu eh- ren ma-

eh- ren ma-   chen,   und   zu eh- ren ma- chen,   ma-

XIX. [Die Warheit ist gen Himel geflogen]

XX. [Aus tieffer noth]

XXI. Psalm. XC

XXII. Dictum S. Augustini

XXIII. Psalm. 119

88

XXIIII. [Si mundus hic demonibus]

89

Ende der 24. Gesenge. *Sit laus Deo.*